THE ROMANCE WRITER'S HANDBOOK

How to Organize and Outline Your Romance Novel

THE ROMANCE WRITER'S HANDBOOK

How to Organize and Outline Your Romance Novel

by LaFlorya Gauthier

Revised Edition

Authors Choice Press
San Jose New York Lincoln Shanghai

LaFlorya Gauthier,

Romance Writer and Author of

"Whispers in the Sand,"

presents

THE ROMANCE WRITER'S HANDBOOK

How to Organize and Outline Your Romance Novel
Revised Edition

Authors Choice Press
an imprint of iUniverse.com, Inc.

For information address:
iUniverse.com, Inc.
620 North 48th Street, Suite 201
Lincoln, NE 68504-3467
www.iuniverse.com

Originally published by GNW Systemed, Inc., Books

ISBN: 0-595-14936-7

Printed in the United States of America

TABLE OF CONTENTS

LESSON 31

WHY Write Romance Fiction?

An Introduction to HOW TO ORGANIZE AND OUTLINE YOUR ROMANCE
NOVEL

Because nearly one million American dollars are spent annually on genre
novels, that's nearly two million paperbacks. What can you, as a new writer
expect to earn? You can earn anywhere from $1,500 to $10,000 and more as an
advance on the sale of your first romance novel depending on what kind it is, who
publishes it and the number of copies printed. Royalties are from 6 to 8% of the
cover price.

And it doesn't take forever to write a romance novel. You could write one
in six months or less, depending on the time you wish to spend each day. I know
writers who use their computers write one novel each month. You say you don't
know anything about writing a romance novel. That's the purpose of this
workbook/handbook. To help you learn how to. Edward R. Murrow, the late
American radio and television journalist encouraged me with my journalism when
he told me that "journalists are made not born." I might add the same thing about
Romance Writers. When you learn to write saleable romance fiction, you learn to
write sensuously, creating vivid word pictures. You will learn to build solid plots,
learn to understand motivation, so that your characters take on depth and

Why Write Romance Fiction?

An Introduction to How to Organize and Outline Your Romance Novel

dimension. And, you will learn to be fresh and·original. You will also learn discipline.

You don't need to have a PhD, to write romance fiction. The editor is interested in how you put words together that takes the reader away from an everyday humdrum life into a lovely world of romance where dreams always come true. In other words you become a dream maker. If you have ever been in love, you have the background you need, and with help, you develop your own romantic style but if you're like me, a romantic at heart, all you need is a little encouragement. For that encouragement, I would like to thank my writing guru, Dr. Ruth Kanin, of Montreal, Quebec, Canada. That's also where I live.

There are no geographical requirements to writing a romance novel. You don't need to travel to the far ends of the earth. Careful research can take care of that if you prefer far off places. But any place can be made romantic. And if you are lucky enough to be living in what I sincerely believe is North America's most romantic city, Montreal, Quebec, Canada, then you have it made.

There are no sex or age requirements either. Although romance writing

Why Write Romance Fiction?

An Introduction to How to Organize and Outline Your Romance Novel

seems to be more suited to women writers, I personally know several men romance writers and others who write with a friend or wife. I don't know if you have ever heard of Jennifer Wilde: The late Tom Huff. Patricia and Clayton Matthews have sold over one million copies of their books. And, everyone knows of the late Princess Diana's late step-grandmother, Barbara Cartland, who recently died at the age of 97. She wrote romance novels for young people until a few years ago.

Best of all, you have a guaranteed readership. The various categories sell each month to the same readers. Romances are selling so fast now that publishers find it difficult to keep up with the demand and with the Far East opening up, the sky's the limit. When I was in the Far East- Singapore, Malaysia, Thailand, China, Hong Kong, etc., it was interesting to see the Harlequin and other familiar logos above Chinese characters! And there's Eastern Europe, South America, Australia, New Zealand and all of Africa, Portuguese, French and English.

Having said that, you see that there is a tremendous market for romance fiction. Silhouette, now a division of Harlequin got there first with the most. In

Why Write Romance Fiction?

An Introduction to How to Organize and Outline Your Romance Novel

their first year, 21 million Silhouette Romances were sold, and that was before they began publishing ethnic romances. They were so impressed with their own success, they published their SPECIAL EDTION in 1982, featuring more sensuality than ever before. Three months later, SILHOUETTE DESIRE became their hottest line. But after doing extensive reader research, SILHOUETTE INTIMATE MOMENTS arrived. With its longer format and increased adventure angle, the love scenes took a greater portion of the story.

Other publishers have developed new romance lines. The original publisher of my novel, **Whispers in the Sand**, is GENESIS PRESS. Inc., who first published it in hardback form in November 1996, then in conjunction with Balllantine's One World line, it was re-issued in pocket book form (mass market) in 1998. And it is still selling on the Internet through Amazon.com and Barnesandnoble.com, to name two who still have it in stock. It can also be ordered directly from Genesis Press, through their website. Genesis Press has expressed an interest in publishing Hispanic and Oriental themed romances. They are always looking for new and interesting manuscripts.

Why Write Romance Fiction?

An Introduction to How to Organize and Outline Your romance Novel

And do you remember Dell Publishing's Candlelight Ecstasy Supreme? The Berkely Publishing Group came out with Second Chance at Love and Bantam did Loveswept. Harlequin Romances are in on this trend with Temptation and Superromance, Harlequin Intrigue, just to name three of their extensive lines. Now imagine for a moment - if you wrote for Harlequin where your books would go. Harlequin books are published in Toronto, New York, London, Amsterdam, Paris, Sydney, Hamburg, Stockholm, Athens, Tokyo, Milan, Madrid, Warsaw, Budapest, Auckland and, of course, distributed even more widely, now that there is Internet and their television division.

What does all of this mean to you? You ask. It means that it's a world wide market, easily accessible because the readers have voracious appetites for new approaches to the same old love story.

Two of the most important changes romances have undergone are probably: one, a direct of the baby-boomers growing into middle age and two: the advent of the belated interest in ethnic romances. The publishing houses are trying to reach today's reader with contemporary settings and heroines. The

Why Write Romance Fiction?

An Introduction to How to Organize and Outline Your Romance Novel

heroine in today's romances is not a nineteen-year old blond virgin. She is older, wiser, more experienced, she is any race, and, she has a good job. She cares about something other than getting married. Although, when she meets the hero, this comes to mind. He is, of course, the one she's been waiting for and who is much more suitable for her than the one she left behind. Ladies and gentlemen this woman has a past!

Athough the hero is magnetic, he doesn't have to be perfect. In fact, most publishing houses like a flaw or two, both in physical make-up and in his personality. All flaws are done away with before the book ends though. The hero is gentle, always a perfect lover and an expert in his career, very successful on all levels. And of course, he is madly in love with the heroine.

Contemporary romance fiction, sometimes known as category fiction is much easier for the new writer and they have erotic scenes. They are written with a formula, if you like. One reader has written, "I took about a dozen of them, folded the corners down on the hot pages and found they occurred at a similar frequency and were of similar duration in the various novels of each line." But

Why Write Romance Fiction?

An Introduction to How to Organize and Outline Your Romance Novel

don't forget that each line is different, so you'll have to do some homework before you set to work. (I"ll tell you how to analyse a novel in a monent). You can also write to the publisher whose line you are interested in writing for asking for a "Tip Sheet," with your Self Addressed Stamped Envelope. A "Tip Sheet" is the publisher's guidelines. These are also now on the Internet.

Berkley and Harlequin's Superromance tips sheets state that it's OK for the hero and heroine to make love before they get married, and that you can describe each scene sensuously, but DON'T YOU DARE use any of THOSE WORDS! Make it poetic and exciting. They also ask for a steady build-up in sexual tension throughout the book.

Publisher's tip sheets are often so meticulously detailed that thy almost write the story for you. If you can write a story at all, you should be able to make a play for this very lucrative market. But if you are queasy about writing erotica, you might want to gingerly ease yourself in by reading "Writing Romance Fiction for Love and Money" by Helene Barnhart. It has a chapter devoted to sensuality and how to achieve it on the page. In a romance novel, the romance comes first,

Why Write Romance Fiction?

An Introduction to How to Organize and Outline Your Romance Novel

then the characters, then the story, and finally the sex.

But in romance writing you will need a whole new list of sensual adjectives because these scenes call for some clever avoidance of clinical terminology. Each publishing house has a different degree of evasiveness, and the writers within those lines also differ in their approach. Some are so vague it's difficult to tell if the writer is talking about the ocean or the heroine when he or she writes of, for instance . . . waves cresting.

Keep in mind that the heroine is always thinking about the hero in a sexual way, even when she's trying not to. But she requires seduction because romance heroines are still "good girls." They don't have sex in between loves, like normal people do. They wait until they fall in love with Mr. Right.

Passion takes a whole different course, because we have over two hundrd pages to follow it, our heroine takes her time with each tender moment.

How to write about sex without mentioning it? How about luminous with desire, mind-drugging kisses, languorous strokes or frenzy of need? You get the idea.

Why Write Romance Fiction?

An Introduction to How to Organize and Outline Your Romance Novel

Above the waist, it's all right for men to have nipples and women to have breasts, but when you get down yonder, the women have depths of passion and the men have hidden fires or surges of passion.

Keep in mind though, that in a romance novel each person has to respect the other or the deal's off.

How to get in the mood to write a good sex scene? Wear a sexy nightgown, light scented candles, move your computer in front of the fireplace or pour a glass of champagne and sip it slowly. Whatever works for you. But what will visitors think of your wearing a nightgown in the middle of the afternoon, or what if your husband gets ideas? "Frankly, all you need to be able to write a good love scene is to enjoy making love yourself. Any good romance writer is a romantic and knows that's one of the best things in life. It should come pretty automatically," Joyce Thies, a romance author says. And who am I to argue?

HOW do I learn? You ask.

Begin by looking at the Title Page of a romance novel tht interest you. Write the title, the author, publisher, date of publication, name of the specific

Why Write Romance Fiction?

An Introduction to How to Organize and Outline Your Romance Novel

romance line, type of romance it is. Now, when you read the book the first time you probably didn't pay too much attention to its structure. You read it because it interested you. Now, go back and ask yourself these questions: Did it hold my attention? Or did it drag in places? What part of the novel interested you the most? Was it background? Characters? Plot? The style or writing? Did you find anything outstanding about the author's work? Sensuous style? Exotic background? What about the dialogue? What will you remember about this novel? Did it evoke an emotional response from you? Did it make you cry? Laugh? Get angry? Did you like the main characters? Maybe you fell in love with the hero. Did the author arouse sensual reactions in you? How would you grade this novel on a scale of one to ten, and, most important of all, would you read this author again?

Characterization is extremely important in romance fiction: in chapter one of the book you're analyzing write the heroine's name, her age, her profession, her position in that profession, her dominant character traits, and a brief physical description. Write a paragraph describing everything you know about her

Why Write Romance Fiction?

An Introduction to How to Organize and Outline Your Romance Novel

background - her family, her education and any special experiences she may have had.

Write a paragraph about what you know about her psychologically and emotionally. Do the same for your hero. Allow less space for your secondary characters,perhaps a paragraph each.

Now for the Plot: Write out what happens in the first chapter and each subsequent chapters. Record all physical action in chapter one. What did they do? What did they say? Did they give each other certain informtion about themselves? Write out the events as they happen. Now, return to the same chapter one. What happened to their emotions? How did they feel about each other as chapter one opens? What about conflict and complications?

In romance fiction there is always strong feelings of ambivalence when the two leading characters meet. They are physically attracted to each other but have strong doubts about each other. There is misunderstanding, often on both sides. And this is compounded when the leading characters are of different cultures and/or nationalities.

Why Write Romance Fiction?

An Introduction to How to Organize and Outline Your Romance Novel

Uncertainty between them is a must in the plot of every romance novel. It is the misunderstanding in the beginning that gives rise to complication after complication as the story unfolds. Each further misunderstanding helps to heighten emotional conflict between them. Based on what you know about the book you are analyzing, What things happen to keep the lovers apart and cause their misunderstanding? List the external complications. These complications can evolve from differences of opinions on issues important to each character. Next, list the inner conflicts that keep them apart. To get a better understanding of the heroine's inner conflict, go back to your novel. Underline in red every phrase that shows the heroine's physical and emotional attraction to the hero. Underline in another color, each phrase that shows her negative feelings toward the hero: whether it's doubt, suspicion, fear or anger.

That is what makes a romance novel work: the heroine's push and pull click click feelings.

Now to the Setting: Describe the setting. How does it add to the sensuality of the story? Was it accurate? Was it romantic by nature? How did the author

Why Write Romance Fiction?

An Introduction to How to Organize and Outline Your Romance Novel

accomplish this? Try to imagine what sources the author used to gather information about the setting. Your own sources, by the way, can be travel agents, chambers of commerce, librarians, magazines, pals videos or the Internet.

What is the hero's attitude toward the heroine's profession, if any? And vice versa? More and more, and especially in love scenes, we have both points of view. If there was a change in points of view what were the author's reasons? Was the book you are analyzing written in multiple points of view? Was the story told through the thoughts of several characters? Did they confuse you?

How sensuous was this novel? Did the author make use of all five senses? Was the author's vocabulary rich enough in words to make you feel sensuous? Go back and circle the words that created the sensual mood of the story. Make a list of the words and phrases, then make a list of words you would have used. By doing this list you will increase your awareness of sense imagery. How would you describe a potential heroine's beautiful hair?

Now to the sex scenes in this novel: How explicit were they? How early did they touch? How soon did they kiss? Was the sexual act consummated?

Why Write Romance Fiction?

An Introduction to How to Organize and Outline Your Romance Novel

How many times? How many pages were allotted to each sex or love scene?

How were they? Tender? Gentle? Passionate? Somewhat explicit? Very

explicit? Did you enjoy them or did they turn you off? Were they in good taste?

As briefly as you can, write the plot of the novel you have analyzed. In a

synopsis you tell how the novel begins, describe the major problem that keep the

lovers apart and what exactly happened to resolve the problem. Then tell how the

novel ends. You will find that writing a short, informative synopsis very useful

when you write your own romance novel.

It is my hope that by the end of your working with How toOutline and

Organize Your Romance Novel you will have been able to write the of the kind of

romance novel you wish to write.

WHEN? You ask.

Now is as good a time as any to start. As you probably know there are

many varieties of romance novels on the market. I write contemporary romance

intrigue, historicals and multi-generational sagas.

However, once you have the category you wish to write for, study it

Why Write Romance Fiction?

An Introduction to How to Organize and Outline Your Romance Novel

carefuly by reading and analyzing it. The best thing you do for yourself is to know your market.

Good luck with your career as a romance fiction writer.

WHAT TO EXPECT FROM THIS HANDBOOK

There are all sorts of "How-to-Write" books on the market today. Many contain instructions on developing plot, character, theme, conflict and resolution. That's all good, but "How-to-Get Started" and keep at it to the end? "How-to-Organize" your thoughts and get them onto your computer screen? "How-to-Integrate" the most important elements of **Your Romance Novel** such as character, plot, conflict and theme? They don't do that.

This Handbook is completely different from all those others out there. First, it's a workbook and a planner. It will help you get your ideas onto your computer screen so that your story doesn't fall apart midway through.

How? If you have an idea for a story but don't know how or where to begin, this workbook/handbook is for you. It will show you how to organize your thoughts. It will lead you through a series of exercises that will help you decide what category of **Romance** you want to write. It will help you set the tone, the setting, the characters, the plot, the conflict, the theme, the beginning and the ending. It will show you how to capture and hold the reader's interest. You will learn "How-to-Build" a powerful and unforgetting climax.

As you work through this workbook/handbook **Your Romance Novel** will take shape and by the time you finish it, you will be ready to write that **Romance Novel** you have only been dreaming about. Once you are writing, you won't wander around or get lost and abandon your story. The time you you spend working through this book will pay huge dividends in the end. Organization will free your creativity.

Writing good **Romance Novels** is an art and a craft. This workbook/handbook will help you develop craft. Your creative powers are freed.

Before we start, perhaps you prefer working directly onto your computer. If so, give your onscreen workbook a title and let's get started . . .

How to integrate all the elements of a **Romance Novel.**

A brief explanation

I wrote the first edition of this handbook because it filled a need for would be first time authors. It was well received and sold well.

With Romance novels accounting for nearly 50% of all mass market paperback sales worldwide, and one being sold every six seconds in the United States alone, why not realize YOUR DREAM of writing a romance novel for this vast market?

Writing the forward for How to Write a Romance for the New Markets Kathryn Falk, Lady of Barrow, writes . . . "Like acting or painting, romance writing is a dream occupation . . ."

Did you know that nearly a hundred and fifty new romances are published each month? And that's just in North America.

Did you know that the average North American reader spends more than a hundred dollars a month on books? (And it was thought that television would kill book sales).

Did you know that the average North American romance reader buys up to forty books a month?

And, best of all, did you know that romance readers enjoy better sex lives?

This revised edition of my handbook is designed to lead you through lessons that will establish the kind of romance novel you plan to write, what your novel is about, the mood it manifests, its culmination, its background and environment, its hero/heroine and supporting characters, how to end your romance novel, how to establish conflict and to resolve it, how to plot and how to grab the reader's interest.

I have labored hard to arrive at writing publishable romance novels. I have made copious notes, countless outlines, written, rewritten and rewritten, polished, reread and repolished my books, short stories and poetry. I would have to be pretty dumb not to have learned something from all those hours at my computer! With this book, I will share what I have learned with you.

I have several reasons for believing that this book is worth your time and money. Organizing and outlining **Your Romance Novel** can save you months of struggle. For the new writer, it is necessary to know where to begin, how to continue and where to end. If this workbook/ handbook enables you to successfully write the romance novel you have always dreamed of, then the time and effort I have put into creating it will be time well spent.

Whenever I have needed examples to illustrate a specific scene, for the most part, I have used my romance novel "Whispers in the Sand", published by Genesis Press, Inc., 315 3rd Avenue North, Columbus, MS 39701, and One World Ballantine, 201 East 50th Street, New York 10022, and soon to be published, "Aminata of Casamance" and "Golden Orchid", "Whispers in the Snow", and "Charlotte's Tree".

Shall we begin?

THE ROMANCE WRITER'S HANDBOOK

How to Organize and Outline **Your Romance Novel**

Detailed ways to develop:

What your story is about

Mood

Background and environment

The hero/heroine and supporting characters

Conflict

Conflict resolution

Plotting

The process of grabbing the reader's interest

How to use *tags* to increase romantic tension

How to create and use sexual tension

Culmination

The end

LESSON 1

DECIDING ON THE CATEGORY

Knowing which category of romance novel you want to write and knowing who publishes it is crucial. Each category caters to a different audience, and each requires a different approach to settings and characters. Knowing as much as possible about the category you are working in will also focus your plotting.

To help you decide what category of romance novel you want to write, attend writer's conferences, if possible. Write to the publishers of the category you're writing for their tipsheets or guidelines or better yet, check out their books in the stores. Copy their websites and visit them. Subscribe to romance periodicals. (See Appendix A at the end of this handbook for addresses of magazines and newspapers and Appendix B for writer's organizations).

Here is a list of possible categories for you to choose from:

Western Romance (North American/Canadian/ United States)

Romantic Suspense

Romantic Adventure

Contemporary
- Multicultural
- Ethnic
Fantasy Romance
- Historical Fantasy
- Urban Fantasy
- Contemporary Fantasy
- Humorous Fantasy
- Science Fantasy
- Dark Fantasy
Romantic Saga

Romantic Mystery

Historical Romance
- Multicultural
- Ethnic
Science Fiction Romance
- Futuristic
- Time Travel
"That fairy kind of writing that depends only upon the imagination" -Dryden

Romantic Intrigue
Young Adult (contemporary)
Superromance (contemporary)
Regency
Gothic
Gay
Inspirational
Foreign Historical Romance

*If you write for guidelines, don't forget to enclose a self-addressed stamped envelope. If you are a Canadian writer writing to American publishers, you can obtain American stamps by writing to an American post office in a nearby town and vice versa for American writers. If writing to foreign publishers, for both American and Canadian writers, buy an International

LESSON 1 continued

Deciding on the Category

Coupon from your local post office. If you have access to the internet and a printer, it is possible to print out guidelines from the website of the publishers that interest you.

However, if your manuscript or enquiry letter is on your hard disk and backed up on a diskette you can simply notify your correspondent that a self-addressed envelope isn't necessary because you have a back up on diskette.

"If you write about the things and the people you know best, you discover your roots. Even if they are new roots, fresh roots . . . they are better than . . . no roots."

- Isaac Bashevis Singer

LESSON 2

GETTING TO KNOW YOUR CATEGORY

Let's take a look at the category of romance novel you want to write.

List and read five published romance novels in the category you plan to write. List the authors.

1.

2.

3.

4.

5.

Describe how these novels are similar. Are their heroes/heroines and supporting characters developed to your satisfaction?

Is the sexual tension between the hero and the heroine obvious from their first meeting?

Is there enough difference between the supporting characters?

Use the space below and the back of this page to explain or if you prefer, use your computer screen.

Why do you read romance novels?

LESSON 2 continued

Getting to Know Your Category

Why do you think other people like to read them?

Use the space below or your computer to list your answers.

Describe how your romance novel will be like the ones you listed.

Describe how it will be different.

LESSON 3

SETTING THE MOOD

Make your work space romantic, it will put you in the proper mood to write sensuously.

Place pictures depicting romantic scenes, or photographs of your favorite film stars who resemble your hero and heroine above your computer to create the atmosphere you need. Place your favorite flowers in a vase beside your computer or printer. Make a collage of your favorite romance novel covers and place it where you can see it while you work. Check out pictures in fashion and women's magazines, in men's periodicals, and newspapers until you find pictures that help you bring your characters to life. Keep the images of your hero and your heroine near your computer.

When you have the Setting you want find pictures that could be it. Do the same for homes and inside rooms. These will help you visualize the world you are creating and keep you there while you are working. Always gaze at the world through rose colored glasses no matter where you are or what you are doing. You never know when your hero, heroine or some other character in your book will appear.

When you have decided which category of romance novel you are going to write, check out their publishers on the internet and print out their guidelines. (You will find publisher's websites in their books which you can copy in bookstores or libraries).

All romance publishers' guidelines set out their specific rules for acceptable heros and heroines, secondary characters, plot, setting and sex scenes.

Characters: Now is the time to make your character biography, full narrative descriptions, of every aspect of your hero and heroine from their faces to their psyches. Save these on your computer, or if you are printing everything, place the hard copies in the appropriately labelled folder. Add any pictures you may use.

Clothing: You should be keenly interested in your heroine's attire since what she wears greatly contributes to her mood, sense of attractiveness and aura of romance. Your readers are always interested in what your characters are wearing. Help can come from pictures in magazines, department store brochures and newspaper advertisements. Clip pictures of models and label this folder clothing. If you are writing a historical romance consult your library or the internet for information about the clothing for the period you are writing about.

LESSON 3 continued

Setting the Mood

<u>Career Information:</u> Depending on the period and cultural aspects of your romance novel your characters differ greatly. In most contemporary romance novels both hero and heroine have careers. In historicals, the culture and period are important. For example: In Spanish cultures women have always owned property and kept their maiden names when married. Children shared both family names. In historical African-American life, and early pioneering life, the women most often worked alongside the men before returning home to do domestic chores.

<u>Food:</u> Dining in a favorite restaurant is always important in many romance novels. Readers like to know exactly what your hero and heroine were eating when they gazed into each others eyes. If you haven't been to the restaurant, read magazine's like Bon Appetit and Gourmet which print menus from famous restaurants, including the proper wine to go along with each serving. Collect menus from posh places you visit on special occasions. (The restaurant owner and maitre d' will be flattered when you explain that you're doing research for **Your Romance Novel**).

But be careful to keep the food, restaurant and drinks appropriate to your particular characters. For example: In "Whispers in the Sand," Momar, the hero, invites Lorraine, the heroine, to lunch on Goree Island where they sample local dishes. He also joins Lorraine and a friend as they are finishing a meal at a local hotel's dining room. As well, his cook prepares a meal for them at Momar's home.

<u>Setting:</u> Use chamber of commerce pictures, articles clipped from magazines, post cards from relatives and friends who travel, maps and brochures from travel agents. Also check out up-to-date travel books from your local library. Visit websites and print them now that they have maps which give details of almost any area you might need.

<u>Furnishings:</u> Create your own interior decorations for the characters you have created. An apartment or a home for a contemporary career woman is different from the drawing room of an English country manor, or a 19th Century African-American slave cabin. For your contemporary North American furnishings, check out some of the following magazines: House Beautiful, Better Homes and Gardens, Sunset, Woman's Day, Family Circle, Ladies Home Journal, Good Housekeeping, Vogue, Town and Country, Architectural Digest, Chatelaine.

Antique Magazine, Antique and Collectors Mart, Antique Monthly and Antique Reader Weekly are all good for period furniture and your public library and the worldwide web are good for foreign furnishings. Since your readers are usually well-versed in such matters, be thorough and accurate in your research.

LESSON 3 continued

Setting the Mood

Chapter Folders: Yes, even with computers you will need folders and hard copies. Label your folders as follows:
- Characters - hero, heroine and supporting characters
- clothing
- hero's professional background
- heroine's professional background
- food
- setting
- furnishings
- plant and animal life
- chapters.

Your Office Space.

In addition to your computer, you will need a printer, a telephone and maybe a FAX machine or perhaps you prefer using the FAX included in your software. It is useful, as well to obtain an e-mail address. Many browsers offer free e-mail addresses now. Check out the one most useful for you.

You will need a filing system for your hard copies.
1.   Files: Label "Research" on this drawer or large folder. File folders on clothing, career, background, etc. behind them in alphabetical order or however you work.

2.   Label a second drawer or large folder with the working title of your romance novel and "Business."

A) Editorial correspondence. If you would rather keep a hard copy file instead of a computerized one, each time you submit your manuscript to an agent or publisher, keep all letters you write and receive in this file. Staple a copy of your letter behind the reply. Keep all correspondence in chronological order. Make a new file folder for each submission.

B) Upgrade and update your guidelines periodically from the Internet or publisher and keep them in a separate file.

C) Keep magazines such as Writer's Digest, Affaire de Coeur and Romantic Times if you like but you can also check out their websites, or consult them at your local library or internet cafes if you haven't a subscription..

LESSON 3 continued

Setting the Mood

D) Keep ideas for future novels in a special file either in hard copy or on your computer. It is also a good idea to always carry a small notepad and pen or pencil in your purse in order to jt down ideas. Keep both near your bed for ideas that come to you in dreams or in the middle of the night.

E) Ongoing business - Label files appropriately.

F) On the Internet you will periodically check agents' websites for updates of their guidelines.

G) You will keep the names of publishing companies, libraries and peoples websites about the research for your current book.

LESSON 4

WHEN DOES YOUR ROMANCE NOVEL TAKE PLACE?

1) Establish the year or period in which your romance novel takes place.

2) What is the time span of your romance novel?

   a) A week?

   b) A month?

   c) Several years?

   d) A saga, covering several generations and centuries?

LESSON 5

WHERE DOES YOUR ROMANCE NOVEL TAKE PLACE?

Knowing the place or places where your story is set is important. Have you either visited or thoroughly researched the setting?

Write a ten line description of each of the locations where your romance novel takes place.

LESSON 6

DEVELOP A DETAILED DESCRIPTION OF WHERE YOUR ROMANCE NOVEL TAKES PLACE.

Know the sites where your romance novel takes place. If you haven't visited them, write to their chambers of commerce, travel agencies or tourist bureaus or go to the internet and type in the setting (city, state, province, country) and once you have it, clock on "map" to get a detailed setting. Print it if you need to. It is no longer necessary to buy maps, study books from your local library in order to get to know the streets, the architecture, the land, lakes, streams and rivers. But you will want to know what the settings look like in winter, in summer, in the autumn and in the spring, at sunset, at sunrise, during the day and at night? For this you will need to study books from your local library or travel brochures or travel magazines.

Get to know what kinds of stores and restaurants there are at the setting. If it is a large city, your local library will probably have newspapers and telephone directories. And the stores and restaurants will most likely include advertising flyers with your local newspaper or in special publicity bags distributed indepentantly. If the setting is somewhere else, write to the town's historical society if they have one or check it out on the internet.

Write a detailed outline, on your computer, or below entitled Settings. Or title it, Lesson 6, Settings if you are doing this on your computer.

Lesson 6a. Describe one place where your romance takes place. It if is a small town, describe the size. What is the population? What is the population like? That is, is it a bedroom community, a suburb, a middle class? Is it ethnically mixed, or one race? Are there any industries? If so, are the industries old or new?

Example: The story takes place in St. Gabriel-de-Brandon, Quebec, a town of about five thousand mostly French-speaking people dominated by the summer tourism industry. It is a sleepy community in winter.

Lesson 6b. What kind of climate does it have in winter, spring, summer and autumn? If your story spans these seasons.

Is it sunny most of the time or does it rain a lot?

Is it hilly, flat, mountainous?

What's nearby: mountains, lakes, rivers, an ocean, a glacier?

What kinds of vegetation grows there?

What kinds of birds are there?

Example: St. Gabriel-de-Brandon, Quebec, is at the edge of the Laurentian Mountain range. The land is very hilly. The mostly evergreen covered Laurentian Mountains tower above the town on the west. On the north, east and west are small farms of oats, wheat and corn. It surrounds the huge Maskinonge Lake to which thousands of summer tourists flock, tripling its population. In winter it is inundated by gros becs, blue jays and numerous other wild birds which have grown accustomed to being fed. They no longer migrate south.

Write your example on your computer under the heading you will use to identify it or write it below.

Lesson 6c. Why have you chosen these settings?

Lesson 6c Continued

Can you make them come alive to your readers?

Try making your settings come alive on this page or on your computer.

LESSON 7

GENERAL AND SPECIFIC LOCATIONS

If your story is taking place in a variety of places:

It will generally have several major general locations, for example:

1.   A particular country or countries

2.   A specific area of a country or countries

3.   Specific city or cities within that country or those countries

      A) a designated house, houses, restaurants, street scenes, streets, transportation

      B) a particular resort, a particular snowmobile trail, a particular road

      C) a particular building, a school, a television or radio studio, a farm

Lesson 7a. Some examples to help you.

1)   A Particular Country: Belgium: A western European country, on the North Sea, bordered by Holland to the north, Federal Germany and Luxemburg on the East, and France to the south. It's 30,500 square kilometers in size and its capital is Brussels. It has nine provinces and its languages are: German, French and Dutch. Its currency is the Belgian Franc.

2)   A Specific Area of a Country: Namur: A south Belgian province of 3,600 square kilometers of three departments or counties. (Dinant, Namur and Phillipesville) and 38 communes. The Sambre and Meuse rivers separate the Ardenne from the extreme north of the province, known for its limestone plateaus where cereal cultivations dominates.

3)   A Specific City: Anvers or Antwerpen: A city in Belgium whose province has the same name. Its population is about 800,000. It was established at the estuary of l'Escaut river on the right and is connected to Liege by the Albert Canal. It is one of Europe's largest port cities and one of Belgium's main industrial centers (metals, automobile factories, petroleum and petrochemical refineries and diamond cutting, etc.).

Lesson 7a continued

General and Specific Locations

A) a designated house: (From "Aminata of Casamance"). The hut was mud with a thatched roof and it was impossible from where they huddled to tell how many rooms there were. It blended so well into its surroundings that one would initially think it was abandoned.

a designated restaurant: (From "Whispers in the Sand"). Lorraine glanced around the restaurant at the richly colored upholstery on the plush chairs and the tables with their matching cloths. Each one had a vase of exotic African flowers in its center. The walls were lined with paintings of Senegalese scenes and murals with jungle motifs. The carpet was thick enough to mute the sound of conversation and clinking silverware.

a designated street scene: (From "Whispers in the Sand"). She surveyed this strange city as she drove, watching the people restlessly as they went about their business despite the downpour. Communal taxis, car rapides, minibuses with passengers hanging precariously on the sides and backs, private cars, carts, bicycles and mopeds all whizzed around her car. Huge throngs of people jammed the sidewalks.

a designated street: (From "Golden Orchid"). They plunged into the Main Street of the village which was bisected by a trunk road slicing through the center, dodging traffic consisting of peddlers gliding by on bicycles, mopeds, in taxis, pedestrians and once in awhile, huge timber laden trailer trucks all of which whizzed past at highway speed.

designated transportation: (From "Golden Orchid"). The bus they took was packed with Malaysians of all stripes, carrying all manner of things from baskets of clothing to live animals and fowl. A hen laid an egg in the lap of the woman sharing Borman's seat, near the window. Her husband shared the seat on the aisle side.

a particular resort: (From "Whispers in the Sand"). Club Mediterranee at Cap Skirring lay before her. The central pavilions, tennis courts, swimming pool, boats at anchor, the nightclub, all came into view as she approached. She slowed as much as possible to take in the sunbathers under colorful parasols; couples strolling along, arm in arm; hammocks slung between palm trees; and gentle waves rolling onto the bleached sands.

Lesson 7a continued

General and Specific Locations

a particular snowmobile trail: (From "Whispers in the Snow"). Danielle walked slowly along the path cleared for snowmobiles, under the dark pines playing games of shadows on the snow banks.

Here and there the leafless maples and snow covered cedars were cellophaned in ice causing the branches to droop into the pristine snow banks. It was as if a fuzzy white fake fur coat had descended on everything, Danielle mused as Waha reconnoitered into deep snow banks, taking gulps of snow and jumping into them.

B) a particular road: (From "Golden Orchid"). The last ten miles of road had been harrowing, hair pin turns and shoulderless. Salleh had negotiated 180-degree bends on the steep road that cut across thickly forested hills. Sometimes she had closed her eyes rather than look at the sheer drops.

C) a particular building: (From "Aminata of Casamance"). The building hovered, at ten in the morning, like a Toma mask Aminata had once seen on a trip to Guinea. It reminded her of a spirit of the bush, the windows and doors like the receding eyes into the dark mass that is the building's interior, the effect is one of confidence, severity, serenity and feral.

a particular school: (From "Aminata of Casamance"). Aminata loved school. It was her only respite from the miserable life at home. The dismissal bell rang. Everyone's eyes swung toward the closed door. Sister Margaritte ignored the girls inside the classroom as well as the sudden bedlam coming from the outside hallway. The sewing class was their last class of the day.

Sister Margaritte slowly, deliberately strolled down each aisle between the desk of each girl. She scrutinized each girl who sat rigidly at her desk. Sister Margaritte ran her class with military discipline and each girl knew that if there was was even a hint of breaching that discipline everyone would be punished and the culprit would receive the wrath of her peers. Sister Margaritte returned to the front of the classroom, a cold smile on her face.

The girls didn't dare breathe.

a particular radio station: (From "Whispers in the Snow"). The red light outside the studio went off. She moved carefully to the chair at the control console vacated by her predecessor. She consulted the thermometer atop one of the CD

Lesson 7a continued

General and Specific Locations

players in front of her which gave the outdoor temperature, then she touched a number on another CD player to the weather forecast theme song. She glanced at the weather forecast, noted the outside temperature, while adjusting the headset to her ears. The station's identification had finished and her own theme song was coming to a close. Seconds later, the weather forecast theme's musical notes chimed at the note where she always turned on microphone number one and waited for the last chimes to die away before beginning the forecast, then the present temperature outside the studio, finishing with the station's address. She replayed the identification for the station. Its notes had hardly faded before the strains of the first song banged out drums, guitars and other instruments followed by a group of voices in sweet wailings of a Tunisian soul song in Arabic.

List your general and specific locations and briefly describe them either below or on your computer.

Lesson 7b. Describe what you consider the most important details your readers would want to know about your specific and particular places.

a) Where is it?/Where are they?

b) What kind of buildings are there? Renaissance? Futuristic?   Modern?

Are they old, deplapidated, dirty, clean? Is there graffiti?

What are the buildings made of? Concrete? Bricks? Wood? Other?

When were they built?

Lesson 7c. If your story takes place in an office building, or a house, draw a floor plan and paste it in front of your computer. Why? As you write, it helps you to better develop your setting if you can actually see it. If your see it, so will your readers. Or you may use a photograph of what you have in mind.

Further, if your software has a drawing program use it to draw your floor plan, print it out and place it where it's visible as you work.

LESSON 8

YOUR HERO, HEROINE AND SUPPORTING CHARACTERS

Write thorough character sketches. It will help you create a full mental picture of each character. It will alsohelp you develop realistic dialogue. Get to know how each character thinks, acts and reacts in any given situation. Get to know them intimately, so that you are able to make them real and believable to your readers.

Regular romance novels have one hero and heroine plus supporting characters, but some categories tend to have a hero and a heroine plus what can be called secondary heroes and heroines along with the supporting characters. However, for all genres the supporting characters are not as well developed as are the hero and heroine. But you must know them well enough to understand why they are in your story.

Lesson 8a. List your hero, heroine and supporting characters by name. Don't worry if at this stage, you don't know all of your characters. You can list them as needed. Develop them in detail, as well.

Hero/Heroine

Supporting characters
(By importance, if you like)

LESSON 9

LET'S DEVELOP YOUR HEROINE

<u>Very Important:</u> Character Sketch. A thorough character sketch is crucial. Here is an outline to help you develop your heroine.

Name: Age:

Birthplace: Birth date:

Nationality: Marital status:

Occupation:

How she looks is very important in a romance novel.

Height: Weight: Build:

Hair color: Style: Length:

Nose: Lips: Eye color:

Eye brows plucked or natural: Does she wear eyeglasses?
                                     If so, what kind? Why does she need them?
Waist:

Are her shoulders slumped or straight?

What is her posture like?

Does she have any birth marks or tatoos?

Does she have physical, mental or emotional scars?

Does she have any handicaps?

Does she have any individual features that would make her stand out in a crowd?

Tip: It is usually a good idea to give her a bit more than the average woman of her race would have to make her stand out.

LESSON 9 continued

Let's Develop Your Heroine

For example: Hebby Roman, writing in Kathyrn Falk's *How to Write a Romance for the New Markets . . . and Get Published* writes: "To make a character 'stand out', and provide greater contrast with most of the . . . characters in your book, make limited use of unusual (but not abnormal) hair or eye color. This is a wonderful way to supply added flair to your manuscript and your characters."

What are her mannerisms? Check 'Yes' or 'No.'

Cocky	Bold	Stable	Secure	Mature
Loud	Calm	Amusing	Happy	Articulate
Conceited	Arrogant	A weirdo	Friendly	Placid
Has a temper		Optimistic	Loving	A giver
A taker		Ambitious	Energetic	Bitter
Friendly		Motivated	Has complexes	
Has phobias		Is an extravert	Is strong	
Is shy		Is timid	Is emotional	
Is insecure		Is immature	Quiet	Nervous
Morose		Depressed	Inarticulate	Modest
Humble		Normal	Aloof	Agitated
Stolid		Pessimistic	Unloving	Unambitious
Languid		Amiable	Unfriendly	Discouraged
Introvert		Weak		

Add any other mannerisms that are descriptive of your heroine.

Lesson 9a.

Getting to Know Her

Think of your heroine as a real person with a job, or lack of one: with pastimes, fears, beliefs, etc. You certainly won't use all this information in your novel but it will help you know your heroine so imtimately that she becomes a real person to you.

1.   What are your heroine's values?

2.   What are your heroine's strongest believes about herself?

3.   What do others believe about her?

4.   What does she believe about other people?

5.   What does she believe about other ethnic groups?

6.   Does the world situation affect your heroine?

7.   How does your heroine handle personal troubles?

8.   How does she handle professional troubles?

9.   How does she handle financial troubles?

Lesson 9a. continued

Getting to Know Her

10.   How does she handle other troubles?

11.   What is her voice like?
       Pleasant?   High pitched?   Low and sexy?

       Does it change depending on the situation?

       Is it fast or slow?

       Does she speak with an accent?

       What are her repetitive words?

       What are her favorite expressions?

12.   What is her family like now?

       What were they like before?

       Were they rich?

       Are they rich now?

       Are they poor?

       Are they middle class?

       Was she born in another country?

       Were her parents born in another country?

       Are there any family traditions?

Lesson 9a. continued

Getting to Know Her

13.   What do the mother and father look like?

        If they are dead, what did they look like?

        Does your heroine look like one of them?

        Which one?

14.   How many brothers and sisters, if any does she have?

        Are there step or half brothers and/or sisters?

        Are there or were there any adopted siblings?

15.   Are there step parents?

        What was her home life like growing up?

16.   What is her home life like now? Describe it.

17.   What is the physical, mental and emotional atmosphere of her home life?

        Physical:

        Mental:

Lesson 9a. continued

Getting to Know Her

Emotional:

18.   What is her lifestyle?

19   Does your heroine have pastimes? If so, what kind?

20.   Is your heroine into sports? If so, what kind?

If not, why not?

21.   What kind of clothes does your heroine wear?

Weird?

Classic?

Casual?

Other?

22.   How does she wear her hair?
(A drawing or photo here might help).

23.   What kind of people does she like to be around?

Lesson 9a. continued

Getting to Know Her

24.   What foods does she like to eat?

25.   What are her favorite drinks?

26.   What is her favorite mode of transportation?

27.   What are her politics?

28.   What are her favorite colors?

29.   Does she like to be around people?

31.   Who are her friends?

32.   Does she entertain?

33.   Does she play a musical instrument?

34.   Does she have a circle of friends, or one or two intimates?

35.   Does she have enemies?

      If so, why?

      If not, why?

36.   Is she religious?

Lesson 9a. continued

Getting to Know Her

Does she believe in a God?

Is she Catholic?   Protestant?   Jewish?   Muslim?   Buddhist?

Hindu?   Agnostic?   Other?

37.   Does she have any strong loves and/or hates?

Why?

38.   What is her present problem?

39.   Outline briefly how it will get worse.

40.   What is the most important thing to know about your heroine?

41.   Write a one-line characterization.

42.   What trait will make your heroine come alive?

Why?

43.   Why is she worth writing about?

Lesson 9a. continued

Getting to Know Her

44. Why is she different from other heroines?

    Why is she similar to other heroines?

45. Do you like her?

    Why?

46. Do you dislike her?

    Why?

47. Will your readers like or dislike her for the same reasons?

48. Heroines who are remembered are those who have strong personalities. Saints, sinners or a combination of both. Why will this heroine be remembered?

49. What kind of work did your heroine do in the past? (If it helps you to clarify this aspect, fill in a job application form for her).

50. What about your heroine's morality? Describe her sex life, her sexual preferences.

51. What about your heroine's intellect?

    Is she an intellectual person or is she of average intelligence?

Lesson 9a. continued

Getting to Know Her

52.   Is your heroine ambitious or not?

Does she have goals?

If so, what are they?

If not, why?

53.   What is your heroine's educational level?

Where did she obtain this education?

54.   Is she involved in charity work?

55.   Is she involved in politics?

56.   Add any additional information you may think of.

LESSON 10

LET'S AMPLIFY MORE DETAILS ABOUT YOUR HEROINE

1.   Why did you choose this person to be your heroine?

2.   Why is she special to you?

3.   Does she remind you of someone you know?

Tip: In delineating characters, it if is someone you know, do make enough physical changes in order to avoid lawsuits.

Lesson 10a. You should know your heroine well enough by now to write a 250 word character sketch. Pick out her striking characteristics and make her come to life. Make her memorable. (Do this on your computer and use your software to count your words). Or do it below.

Lesson 10a. continued.

Let's Amplify More Details About Your Heroine.

Use the additional space below.

LESSON 11.

TIME TO DEVELOP YOUR HERO.

Character Sketch. Here again, a thorough character sketch is crucial. Here is an outline to help you develop your hero.

Name: Age:

Birth place: Birth date:

Nationality: Marital status:

Occupation:

How he looks is very important in a romance novel.

Height: Weight:

Build: Hair color: style/length:

Nose: Eye color/eye brows:

Beard/mustache/sideburns: Does he wear eyeglasses?

Lips: If yes, what kind?

Waist: Why does he need them?

Are his shoulders broad, narrow, in between, slumped?

What is his usual posture?

Does he have any birthmarks?

Does he have any physical, mental or emotional scars?

What are the individual features that would make him stand out in a crowd?

Lesson 11a. continued

Time to Develop Your Hero

What are his mannerisms?

Cocky	Shy
Bold	Timid
Stable	Emotional
Secure	Insecure
Mature	Immature
Loud	Quiet
Calm	Nervous
Amusing	Morose
Happy	Depressed
Articulate	Inarticulate
Conceited	Modest
Arrogant	Humble
A weirdo	Normal
Friendly	Aloof
Placid	Agitated
Has a temper	Stolid
Optimistic	Pessimistic
Loving	Unloving

Lesson 11a. continued

Time to Develop Your Hero

Giver	Taker
Ambitious	Unambitious
Energetic	Languid
Bitter	Amiable
Friendly	Unfriendly
Motivated	Discouraged
Extravert	Introvert
Strong	Weak

Add any other mannerisms that would make your hero stand out in a crowd.

Lesson 11b.

Getting to Know Him.

Think of your hero as a real person with a job or lack of one: with pastimes, fears, beliefs, etc. You won't necessarily use all this information in your novel, but it will help you to know your hero so intimately that he becomes a real person to you and if he is a real person to you, then he will be so to your readers.

If your hero is a conservative, explain. Give as many examples as you can.
(One example: He is so conservative that he abhors the day women were given the vote).

Your examples:

1.   What are your hero's values?

2.   What are your hero's strongest beliefs about himself?

3.   What do others believe about him?

4.   What does he believe about other people?

        What does he believe about other ethnic groups?

5.   Does the world situation affect your hero?

6.   Why?

        Or why not?

Lesson 11b. continued

Getting to Know Him

Is he involved in politics?

Is he involved in charity work?

7.   How does your hero handle personal trouble?

8.   How does he handle professional trouble?

9.   How does he handle financial trouble?

10.   How does he handle other trouble?

11.   What is his voice like?   Is it pleasant, low and sexy?

        Does it change depending on the situation?

        Is it slow or fast?

        Does he speak with an accent?

        What are his repetitive words?

        What are his favorite expressions?

12.   What is his family like?

        If they are dead, what were they like?

        Are they rich now?

Lesson 11b. continued

Getting to Know HIm

Were they ever rich?

Are they poor?

Are they middle class?

Was he born in another country?

Were they born in another country?

Are there any family traditions?

13.　What do the mother and father look like?

Does your hero look like them?

14.　How many brothers, sisters, if any does or did he have?

Are there step or half brothers and/or sisters?

Are there or were there any adopted siblings?

15.　Are there step parents?

16.　What is his home life like? Describe it.

17.　What is the physical atmosphere of his home life?

What is the mental atmosphere of his home life like?

What is the emotional atmosphere of his home life like?

Lesson 11b. continued

Getting to Know Him

18.   What is his lifestyle?

19.   Does your hero have pastimes? If so, what kind?

20.   Is your hero into sports?

If so, what kind?

If not, why not?

21.   What kind of clothes does your hero wear?

Weird?   Classic?   Casual?

22.   How does he wear his hair?

23.   What does he like to read?

24.   What kind of people does he like to be around?

25.   What foods does he like to eat?

26.   What are his favorite drinks?

Lesson 11b. continued

Getting to Know Him

27.   What is his favorite mode of transportation?

28.   What are his politics?

29.   What are his favorite colors?

30.   What kind of art does he like?

31.   Does he like to be around people?

32.   Who are his friends?

33.   Does he entertain?

        Does he play a musical instrument?

34.   Does he have a circle of friends, or one or two intimates?

35.   Does he have enemies?   If so, why?

        If not, why not?

36.   Is he religious?

        Does he believe in a God?

        Is he Catholic?   Protestant?   Jewish?   Muslim?   Hindu?   Other?

Lesson 11b. continued

Getting to Know Him

37.   Does he have any strong loves and/or hates?

38.   What is his present problem?

        Or problems?

39.   How will it (they) get worse?

40.   What is the most important thing to know about your hero?

41.   Write a one-line characterization.

42.   What trait will make your hero come alive?

        Why?

43.   Why is he worth writing about?

44.   Why is he different from other similar heroes?

45.   Do you like him?

        Why?

        Or, do you dislike him?

Lesson 11b. continued

Getting to Know Him

Why?

46.   Will your readers like or dislike him for the same reasons?

47.   Heroes who are remembered are those who are strong in some way: saints, sinners or a combination of both. Why will this hero be remembered?

48.   What kind of work did your hero do in the past? (If it helps you to make this clearer, fill in a job application form for him).

49.   What about your hero's sex life?

       What are his sexual preferences?

50.   What about your hero's intellect?

       Is he an intellectual person?

       Or is he of average intelligence?

Lesson 11b. continued

Getting to Know Him

51.   Is your hero ambitious or not?

What are his goals?

52.   What is your hero's educational level?

Where did he obtain his education?

53.   Add any additional information you may think of.

Lesson 11c.

The Hero/Heroine Tell the Story (point of view).

Let's look at point of view in contemporary romances. First of all, let's define point of view. Your hero or heroine is the point of view character because of what is happening to him or her. It is necessary to establish the hero or heroine's point of view as soon as possible. In the first two or three paragraphs try to establish name, location, what her or she looks like, and extremely important -- his or her inner thoughts and feelings. You want your readers to identify with the main character as soon as possible.

I begin "Whispers in the Snow" thus:
"You just made it!"

Danielle Garon ran her hand through her short black curly hair. "I know. Thank goodness the road grader came along and cleared our road. Otherwise, even Suki wouldn't have been able to get out of our driveway," she said out of breath. She had broken into a trot in order to arrive in the studio on time.

Julien, the program director at the radio station, patted her companionably on the shoulder, showing her that he sympathized with her. The snow storm the day before had left more than ten feet of snow in the area. He also knew Suki was her beloved Suzuki Samourai four-wheel-drive jeep. Danielle was one of the few people Julien knew who gave names to their cars. She even talked to hers. Julien chuckled remembering the first time he had ridden in Danielle's jeep and heard her conversation with it.

Romance novels generally use third person, singular narration, which exposes all of the character's feelings and thoughts. The author's descriptions are "he" and "she" instead of "I". However, this forces you as the writer to live the story through your hero or heroine and thus forces your reader to do the same, but you gain a feeling of immediacy.

For example: If your heroine is kneeling she has to look up, you look up with her. Or if she is blushing, you feel the blush with her although she doesn't see it unless she sees herself reflected in a mirror or another reflecting object. Say, she's sitting at her table drinking her morning coffee or tea. She can see herself reflected in the tea or coffee pot. This technique is not often used these days.

In romance fiction your heroine is usually your point of view character if it's single point of view you're using. Why is this, you ask? Simply because most of your romance readers are women and they identify with her.

Lesson 11c. continued

The Hero/Heroine Tell the Story

A note of caution: Before you begin your romance novel decide from whose point of view you are going to write. Whatever point of view you choose you must always keep your heroine as the main focus.

Single point of view: When using single point of view, at no time can you enter any others thoughts, or any information that the heroine could not have seen, heard or experienced. All information must be from her point of view as she sees herself, or thinks of herself. (This technique is often used in contemporary romance novels).

Third person point of view is effective for your love scenes.

Example: From "Whispers in the Sand". He leaned toward her, and she could feel him trembling throughout his body. Her own body trembled, too, and she felt like a drum somebody had hit very hard. She turned her willing mouth to him and he took it, easily. His warm, soft lips touched hers in a sweetly seductive kiss.

Helene Schellenberg Barnhart's book, "Writing Romance Fiction for Love and Money has this to say about Viewpoint in Fiction. "Every story has a hero or heroine. If it is written in single viewpoint, that is, from one person's viewpoint only, it is most often the heroine or hero through whom the story flows. Everything that happens is told as that one character sees it, hears it, feels it, or thinks about it. Since the reader identifies with the viewpoint character, he or she cares about what is happening in the story to the same degree that the viewpoint character does.

Shifts in point of view: You may shift point of view briefly into the hero's point of view to give your readers a glimpse of how he feels in a tender or passionate moment. Keep in mind though, that the line for which you are writing will most likely tell you, in their guidelines whose point of view they prefer.

Here is an example of the hero's point of view: From "Whispers in the Sand".
Momar frowned into his mirror and grimaced at his bloodshot eyes. He had not slept a wink. He wondered what had gotten into him last night. He had acted like a hick. "Miss Barbette must think I am an uncivilized boor." He grimaced again. She was not even his type. "I do not even like tall, thin, 'string bean' women." He laughed, not even convincing himself.

Multiple points of view: Mutiple points of view are used when you're writing an historical romance, an historical series, a family saga or one of those long mainstream novels where the action takes place over decades and involves many characters. My

Lesson 11c. continued

The Hero/Heroine Tell the Story

"Aminata of Casamance" and "Charlotte's Tree" are examples. "Charlotte's Tree" is a saga and "Aminata of Casamance" is a long mainstream novel.

It is necessary to keep in mind that although multiple points of view allow you to enter the thoughts of many characters, keep in mind your main character always predominates. It is always his or her story. All supporting characters exist only to shed light on your main character.

Let's look at the omniscient point of view which goes into the minds of various other characters to show their reactions to the hero or heroine or one another.

An example of the omniscient point of view is the "Unknown Mr. Brown" by Sara Seale (Harlequin Romance). Let's see the heroine through another character's eyes.

"Understood what?"
"The arrangements that have been made for your future," the lawyer replied impatiently. Really! The child could look almost half-witted at times with that wide, unblinking stare and the mousy hair dragged back from those prominent ears, giving her a skinned appearance.

Changing point of view is more often used in longer romance novels. Suspense can be created when you show how one character sees the situation. Often we can learn something that character should know and doesn't.

You can switch from one point of view to another gracefully if you change at a break in your story. For instance, at the beginning of a chapter and staying with that character for the entire chapter.

LESSON 12

YOUR SUPPORTING CHARACTERS

You may have several or many supporting characters, depending on the length of your romance novel. While they add depth to your story, they are not developed as fully as are the hero and heroine. Nevertheless, you want to know them well. Return to Lesson 8a where you listed your hero and heroine and supporting characters by name. Develop them in order of importance.

First Supporting Character: Female: Do the same character sketch as you did for your heroine.

First Supporting Character: Male: Do the same character sketch as you did for your hero.

Second Supporting Character: Female: Do a smaller character sketch for her.

Second Supporting Character: Male: Do a smaller character sketch for him.

Subsequent Supporting Characters: Male and female children. Do even smaller character sketches for them.

Pets are also supporting Characters: The can dogs, cats, birds, horses, or anything you like. It depends on what your characters like. You will clip your supporting character sketches to your work book or label them in your computer.

Use the space below for your pet's character sketches.

Lesson 12a.

A Brief Character Sketch for main supporting characters

Now is the time to do a brief character sketch of 100 words for each of your supporting characters. Use the questions supplied for your hero and heroine as a base and add anything else you would like to.

Use the space below or use your computer..

Lesson 12b.

A Brief Character Sketch for Subsequent Supporting Characters

Do a brief character sketch for subsequent supporting characters, including any pets used in your story.

Use the space below or use your computer.

Lesson 12c.

Your Character Sketch Check List

1.   Does each character have a suitable name?

2.   Is each name different from the others?

3.   Is each character individualized so that he or she doesn't resemble another in personality or physically - - unless it has a story purpose?

4.   Is each character developed fully enough?

5.   Does each character give the illusion of reality, of an actual living being - - unless the story demands the opposite?

6.   Is each character necessary to the story?

7.   Does each character use dialogue individual to that personality, so that there is a variety of speech?

8.   Have you given adequate descriptions of each character, physically and psychologically, as well as, in speech and action?

9.   Will the audience care about and root for your hero and heroine? Will the audience have strong feelings against the antagonists?

LESSON 13

THE PLOT

Let's say someone is sitting beside you on the metro or bus and they are getting off at the next stop. They ask: "What is your story about?"

You have to answer, fast. Write in three sentences: the plot (action, or what happens), and the aim of your story (the theme).

Example: In "Whispers in the Sand", my story is about an ambitious female documentary film producer who gets the chance of a lifetime to do a film in a far away exotic country. She falls madly in love with a diplomat from the country, but when a member of her film crew commits a serious crime, she flees. But since the aim is that love conquers all, the hero finds her and they marry.

"Aminata of Casamance". This the story of the most successful metisse international fashion model in the world who builds the greatest fashon and jewelry empire on three continents. But she can never forget the horrors of her childhood in Senegal or the plots of her enemies to destroy her. In spite of everything, she and love triumph.

"Whispers in the Snow" is the story of a thirty year-old Haitian/French-Canadian widow with a small son, a Samourai jeep and a Samoyed dog. She works at a local radio station where the owner complicates her life almost to the breaking point. But since this is a love story, they fall in love, marry and have a baby.

"Golden Orchid" is the story of a Mayalsian/French-Canadian woman who learns when her father dies that the Malaysian mother she has always thought of as 'dead' is very much alive and living in Malaysia. When she sets out to find her all hell breaks loose. But with the help of the hero, not only does she find her mother, but she also finds love.

Now write your examples either below or on your computer.

LESSON 14

LET'S DEVELOP YOUR PLOT

Let's see what happens to your story. Pay attention to two important things:

What happens?

What is the sequence of events?

The first thing to do is:

List the most important events in chronological order.

List them below or on your computer.

Example: In "Whispers in the Sand" Lorraine Barbette is born in Mound Bayou, MS and becomes a documentary film producer. On her first important assignment a member of her film crew commits a serious crime on location. She is so ashamed that she flees the country but she has fallen madly in love with a diplomat from the country. He pursues her and they marry. She forms her own film company.

"Whispers in the Snow." Danielle Caron is born in St. Didace, Quebec, Canada where she grows up, marries and is widowed. Following the loss of her husband, she finds work at the local radio station where the owner and she meet. He has serious psychological problems brought on by an incident while her was in Africa. Danielle has many problems to contend with, including the death of her uncle, the care of her young cousin and Phillipe's (the hero) problems. But gradually everything works out in their favor and they marry.

"Golden Orchid." Lise Deschamps is a Malaysian/French-Canadian woman born in Kuala Lumpur and raised in Montreal. When her father dies she learns that the mother she had been told all her life was dead is very much alive and living in Malaysia. With the help of one of her father's students, Salleh RahimYusif she sets out to find her

LESSON 14 continued

Let's Develop Your Plot

      mother. However, others have severe reasons for stopping her. Nevertheless, with the help of Salleh she triumphs and they find love.

      Now write your example below or on your computer.

LESSON 15

LET'S GET ON TO THE DETAILS OF YOUR PLOT

One of the reasons I wrote this book is to supply you with as many lessons and examples as possible to help you write **your romance novel.** So, here, you probably need a little more direction than just a general plot. (Lesson 13).

Let's do an outline to keep you on track.

In your outline, for example, make realistic preparations for sex scenes. Know your hero and heroine well enough to know what sexual excitement is in it for each one. Try to create sexual actions and reactions in each scene.

Here is one example I used in a scene from "Whispers in the Sand."
"Shivers of excitement raced through her as his fingers caressed the smoothness of her face, moving down to her slender neck."

Another example from "Golden Orchid".
She began a nervous laugh, but only had time for a gasp as his mouth found hers. Lise felt his tongue touch her lips before it went further. His body pressed against hers and she felt the hunger in the hardness of his. His urgent hand slid under her shirt in a gliding motion.
"Salleh," she sighed. "No."

An example from "Whispers in the Snow."
Suddenly the kiss changed and was completely sexual, a man and a woman on fire.
She stopped thinking, only feeling, and her actions urged him to do likewise. They were as alone as they could be in a hospital. Phillipe slid his arms behind her knees and lifted her. Her head rested on his shoulder. She could feel the heat of his neck, his hair.

Make your preparations for sex scenes below or on your computer.

Lesson 15a.

Character Tags

Make use of character *tags* -- words and phrases to establish your characters in the reader's mind. *Tags* are adjectives and phrases that give clues to your character's apearance and important inner feelings.

In selecting character *tags* for your hero and heroine return to their character sketches and develop concrete images that will zero in on such things as their body types, their facial features, their voices, their mannerisms and gestures, etc.

Dress them so as to give clues about their appearances but also their lifestyles and economic levels, their images of themselves.

Choose phrases for both that will let the reader know their state of mind, what they are thinking about each other. By the end of the first chapter your readers should have a good idea of the kinds of people you are writing about.

Here are some examples I used in "Whispers in the Sand."

Lorraine, the heroine

Tags defining her appearance, lifestyle and character	*Tags* of her emotional and psychological state
Honey colored skin	Tired, disturbed, sad, distracted
Hair thick, black, long	Senegal turning point in her life
Well manicured fingernails	Pure joy on arrival in Senegal
Dove gray eyes	Feeling of being relaxed
Film producer with ambitions	
Won scholarship, smart	
Calls off engagement	
Speaks French, well educated	
Pursues ambition	
Takes luxury bath in preparation for reception in honor	Used to pampering herself

Lesson 15a. continued

Character Tags

Momar, the hero

Tags defining his appearance, lifestyle and character	*Tags* defining his emotional and psychological state
I'm a diplomat	Momar Diallo was fuming
Given a confidential assignment because	Snappish, angry
he can be trusted	Congratulates himself on job well-
Black bold eyes, black skin	done
Hair is velvety darkness	Ambitious, wants post in
Long legged	prestigious country
Delivers object of assignment	Feels he deserves posting
to ministry back in Dakar	Furious at another escorting
	asignment
Stalks to car	Angry
Stomps on gas pedal	Decided American film crew he
	is to escort only looking for
	sensations.

Lesson 15b.

Let's Outline Your Plot in Detail.

Create a left column and a right column on your computer screen or use the one below. But for now we're only going to use the left one. We'll use the right one later to show you how to integrate the conflict and sexual tension as well as your *tags*.

If your publisher asks for an outline and sample chapters, this is it! By dong this lesson you are putting yourself ahead of the competition!

List Plot Details (in outline)	Conflict, sexual tension and *tags* (fill this in later)

LESSON 16

THE ULTIMATE GRABBER! HOW TO BEGIN YOUR ROMANCE NOVEL

As an "unknown" writer, most publishers or agents won't give you much of a chance. If you do not capture the reader in the first few paragraphs, you are lost. Editors and agents read manuscripts with this in mind. The sale of **Your Romance Novel** depends on this. But how can you do it?

Spend a lot of time thinking about your story. Begin with an interesting setting, a predicament or an unusual idea.

Lesson 16a. List five interesting ways you could start **Your Romance Novel.** Here are some examples to help you.

An Interesting Setting: Here's how I began "Whispers in the Sand."
Momar Diallo was fuming. He could no longer hold back his resentment. Snarling under his breath, he spoke out.
"Damn it, I'm a diplomat, not a diplomatic courrier or a diplomatic escort!"

The chauffeur turned around in the front seat of the air-conditioned luxury car. "What sir?"

"Nothing," Momar snapped, fearing he would explode with anger.

A Predicament: "Aminata of Casamance."
Aminata had no trouble slipping away without her chauffeur in her glossy black limousine. She had sent him on an errand in the jeep which would take most of the night. He had to go to Casamance to fetch what she'd ordered.

She heard the whine of the sleek executive jet before it broke the light cloud cover and glided to a perfect landing not a hundred feet from her.

The man she was waiting for exited almost before the airplane had come to a complete stop.
Once inside the car he handed her a folded check in the amount she had mentioned earlier on the telephone.

She shook her head slowly now. "I am sorry. I have changed my mind. I can't take it. It's no longer the most important reason I telephoned you."

Lesson 16a. continued

<u>An Unusual Idea:</u> "Golden Orchid."

"Oh Mr. Yusof, may I ask you to do something for me?" Lise cried, almost dropping her cup of tea.

"Of course, but please do not call me mister. My name is Salleh. What may I help you with?" He enquired, curious.

Lise took the manila envelope from a top drawer of the desk and passed it to him without opening it.

"Open the envelope and tell me what the documents inside say, would you please? I think they are written in Malay which I don't read or speak, unfortunately."

"But you are half Malay, are you not?" Salleh asked, opening the envelope.

"Yes, I am but Papa brought me from Malaysia when I was a baby. And I have never had any contact with my mother's people." she explained.

"What does it say? What is in it?" Then she held her breath.

"Shall I tell you about the other two documents?" Salleh questioned gently. He wanted to hold her, to protect her from what he knew the other documents would reveal.

"This marriage certificate was made out in 1965 to Professor Pierre-Yves Deschamps and Keemasan Orchid. The other one is a notice of a divorce dated 18 June 1968."

"That means my mother might still be alive?"

"What do you mean?" Salleh asked.

"Papa and his family always told me that my mother had died when I was born!"

"She would be forty-six now! That's young. I'm sure she's still alive! But how can I find out?"

"What are you going to do?"

"What would anyone in my place do? I'm going to Malaysia to find my mother!"

Lesson 16b. Now, write why the opening idea you chose would interest your readers.

Lesson 16c. Write your opening paragraph, below or on your computer and put is aside for a day or two.

Does it seem as interesting as when you wrote it? If so, proceed. If not, go on with **Your Romance Novel** and come back to the beginning later. Jot down any interesting openers that come to mind while you are continuing with your writing.

LESSON 17

KEEP YOUR READERS TURNING THE PAGES

You have your readers hooked, now keep them turning the pages! How do you do this? By action, believable character development, increased conflict, increased sexual tension, and using more sensual *tags.*

Lesson 17a. Now is the time to review your plot. Think of ways to capture your reader's interest. Summarize each chapter by writing what you feel will make your readers keep reading!

Here are some examples from "Aminata of Casamance."

Chapter number	What Will Keep Them Reading?
Last paragraph of chapter two	"That is only the beginning of what I have in store for you Aminata. Just wait!" She burned with anticipation.
End of chapter three	And it was all super secret. He folded the newspaper neatly with a calmness he was far from feeling. And in doing so, missed the most important piece of news of his entire career.
End of chapter four	Here was a photo of one of the most beautiful women he had ever seen. What a waste to have to kill her but a contract was a contract and that was his business. He had carried out contracts the world over. He wsn't known as 'the snake' for nothing. And Aminata of Casamance hadn't a chance against him.

Lesson 17a. continued

Keep Them Turning the Pages. Use the space below or your computer

Chapter number   What Will Keep Them Reading?

LESSON 18

WHAT IS THE CONFLICT?

Conflict is what makes good romantic fiction. It keeps your readers turning the pages.

In a Romance Novel your conflict can be:

Person vs. Person
Person vs. Himself/herself
Person vs. Nature

or:

Person vs. Person
A Man vs. Another Man
A Woman vs. Another Woman
A Man or Woman vs. Many Men or Women
Men or Women vs. Men or Women (competition)

or:

Person vs. Himself/Herself
One Man vs. Himself (internal conflicts)
One Woman vs. Herself (internal conflicts)

or:

Person vs. Nature
Man or Woman vs. Elements
Man or Woman vs. Hostile Environments
Man or Woman vs. Animals

or:

Combinations of the above.

Lesson 18a. What is the main conflict in **Your Romance Novel?**

In many romance novels of today there can be several conflicts. What are they in your story? List them below or on your computer.

Lesson 18b. Write the conflicts, sexual tension and *tags* in your story.

Here is an example of person vs. Person conflict from "Whispers in the Sand."
Lorraine struggles against her crooked film crewman, Sam, to protect the integrity of her documentary film company and her own professional reputation as well as her love for Momar.

Here is another example of Sexual Tension from "Whispers in the Sand."
His eyes left her face and fell to her neck and further down. Lorraine's sense of excitement swelled. Momar feasted on her more boldly than he had done in the airplane. Lorraine was more firmly bewitched than she had ever been in her life. His presence was overpowering.

Now write your examples below or on your computer.

LESSON 19

HOW CAN YOU RESOLVE CONFLICT, SEXUAL TENSION AND *TAGS*?

Unlike real life, you are in the driver's seat here. You can reach a resolution. Review the stories and novels you have read and liked. How were their conflicts, sexual tensions and *tags* resolved?

How will **Your Romance Novel's** conflicts be resolved?

Here's what happened in "Whispers in the Sand."

Lorraine flees, but her lover follows her and they are married.

Write a one-sentence resolution.

LESSON 20

WHEN SHOULD YOU RESOLVE CONFLICT, INCREASE SEXUAL TENSION AND USE *TAGS?*

Conflict should be established in the first chapters and continue to as near the end as possible.

Sexual tension and *tags* should be used throughout.

Review Lesson 15. Your Outline. When did you indicate conflict resolution, sexual tensions, and *tags?*

If you have ended conflict too early, your readers will feel cheated.

Determine the point at which your conflict is resolved, your sexual tension at its height and an example of a *tag* you could use.

LESSON 21

NOW TO INTEGRATE YOUR PLOT, CONFLICT, SEXUAL TENSION AND *TAGS*

This is essential. Scenes that do not advance the conflict, retain sexual tension and include *tags* are useless. Return to Lesson 15.

At the beginning of each chapter describe how the conflict is evolving.

Describe how you prepare for sexual tension and *tags*.

What is taking place?

What is the action?

What are the events?

What can you use to bring out the conflict?

What can you use to increase the sexual tension?

What can you do to make your *tags* more sensual?

Now is the time to use that right hand column back in Lesson 15b, page 76.

LESSON 22

MAKE YOUR CONFLICT RESOLUTION AND SEX SCENES REALISTIC

Don't try to fool your readers. There is always someone out there who is an expert on what you are writing about. You wouldn't have a skinny, short Betty who is a logger's boss lady and who cuts down as many trees as her crew, who curses like a sailor and who makes love like a wild cat, without giving her some special attributes which makes it possible for her to do such things, now would you?

In other words, if she can do all those things, show why.

Lesson 22a. Now is the time to outline just how your conflict is to be resolved. Begin with a "Statement of Conflict." Next, list the actions and thoughts that lead up to a successful resolution.

In a romance novel, the hero or heroine or both control the conflict in the end. But what is his or her state of mind that leads to change?

What actions help the hero/heroine to overcome opposition?

Your "Statement of Conflict."

Lesson 22b. Does the conflict resolution seem real to you? List five different ways this conflict could have been resolved. Choose the one that seems most real to you.

1.

2.

3.

4.

5.

LESSON 23

WHAT YOUR STORY IS REALLY ABOUT

Describe **Your Romance Novel.** Your publisher will want to know what it's about. Make it exciting. Do it now.

Lesson 23a. Write an actual scene that demonstrates the conflict in **Your Romance Novel.**

LESSON 24

LET'S PUT IT ALL TOGETHER

When **Your Romance Novel** is finished you will find that most romance publishers will ask for a snyopsis and sample chapters. They rarely ask for sketches of your hero and/or heroine, but, in case they do, your are ready.

Now is the time for you to write your synopsis.

It should be a real grabber (but faithful to your story. No lies).

It should be a description of your novel which includes the plot, a cameo of the hero and heroine plus the next two supporting characters, one example or more of sexual tension and at least one *tag* and the conflict.

How to begin?

Here are three examples to help you. The synopsis of "Golden Orchid."

"Golden Orchid" is a contemporary romantic intrigue which takes place in Montreal, Singapore and Malaysia.

The heroine is a twenty-seven year old Malay-French-Canadian television researcher and lives in Montreal. She learns her Malay mother might still be alive when she discovers her mother's young age as listed on the original birth certificate she finds among papers in her father's safe when he dies suddenly. This is further strenghtened when she finds their divorce papers as well, proving her mother hadn't died at her birth as she has been told by her father and his family.

He had renamed her Lise when he returned with her, as a baby, to Montreal. But when the hero translates her birth certificate she learns her original name was Imas Itu or Golden Orchid.

Salleh peered at one of the documents, holding it in his well formed brown hand.

Lise wondered how that beautiful brown hand opening the envelope would feel caressing her cheek.

Salleh had stolen a glance at the young womand and wished it was her lovely hand he was holding instead of the official-looking paper.

Armed with the address on the birth certificate and divorce papers, Lise sets out to find

LESSON 24 continued

Let's Put It All Together

her mother in Malaysia with the help of the hero and against the wishes of her aunt and uncle, her only relatives in Canada.

The hero, Salleh, is a twenty-eight year old aristocratic Malaysian businessman who helps his father run the family's international businesses and was one of Lise's father's graduate students. It is he who translates these important papers for her after she has contacted her father's ex-colleague for help in doing so. That contact, unknown to her, creates the most horrifying episodes in her life.

After an emotional pilgrimage to a shrine in Singapore Lise feels strong enough to forgive her Canadian family for their deception and face anything she might find in Malaysia but nothing could have prepared her for the horrors she and her hero have to face there.

"I am truly sorry Miss Deschamps. But the address given here is now a factory. You see," he went on, Petaling Jaya, where this address is, has grown tremendously in the past tweny years of or. . ." Lise lost track of what he was saying because of the ringing in her ears.

". . . It *has been* over twenty-five years. . ." he was saying.

"But, but my mother!" Lise croaked.

"I am so sorry we cannot help further." He said, standing, holding out his hand. The interview was over.

After discovering her mother's last address in Petaling Jaya, a suburb of Kuala Lumpur, is now an abandoned factory she is somewhat cheered when Salleh, the hero, invites her to a sumptious lunch to cheer her up.

Toward the end of the meal he is duped into leaving her to finish the meal alone. To both their horror she's kidnapped by one of her half brothers who think he's holding her for ransom while her late father's ex-colleague with whom he's involved with in operating illegal businesses has other ideas.

The ex-colleague, Borman, has hated her father for years for what he considers a betrayal and has given the order to her half brother to hold her. Unbeknowest to the brother, Borman, has hired a professional assassin to kill her.

LESSON 24 continued

Lets Put It All Together

Lise tiptoed to the door. She put her ear to it but couldn't hear a thing. Even the insects were quiet. She eased the door open and noticed there was a perceptual difference in the intensity of the light. It was near dawn. She slipped out the door and stood for a moment listening. She heard nothing. She stepped off the last step and headed down a path in the direction of the village.

The killer, dressed completely in black, stopped momentarily, to double check the switch blade. He smiled a lopsided smile, caressing the blade.

Borman had said the front door, where she was being held, had been left unlocked and she was alone.

He was only a few hundred yards away. He moved swiftly, deftly, nimbly.

She had hardly gone twenty yards when she glimpsed someone headed in her direction on the path.

She foils them and with the hero they both elude the kidnapper and the hired assassin only to run out of gas and find themselves stranded at a bed and breakfast, rural Malaysian style.

Lise turned her back to him and the water and counted to ten. Nothing. No sound. She turned around and opened her eyes. Salleh was a foot away from her, his shirt gone. So was his smile.

"You were supposed to be in the water!" She gasped.

She stared at his chest. It was covered with the same blue black hair with flecks of white, as that on his head.

"I thought you mihgt need help." He moved toward her.

Having no news from Lise and feeling exceedingly guilty for their part in the deception about her mother, her aunt and uncle decide to go to Kuala Lumpur and look for her. Once in Kuala Lumpur they learn that Borman is also there, and, is looking for Lise.

The kidnapping proves one thing to Lise. Her mother is alive because the half brother bragged to her that he was holding her for ransom as payment for the grief his family has caused him. She's more determined than ever to find her mother now.

LESSON 24 continued

Lets Put It All Together

The half brother, Abdullah, is determined to hold her because it was the mother who was instrumental in having the family disown him because of his illegal activities which have brought shame upon the family name.

What Lise doesn't know is Borman has had her followed ever since she left Montreal.

Borman only wants revenge on the daughter now that her father can no longer be touched and since she has left the protection of Canada he thinks it will be much easier to have her killed in Malaysia. He's convinced Lise's father kept secret diaries of Borman's illegal activities when they were colleagues in Malaysia working for the Canadian government. He's convinced himself that Lise must have discovered these diaries when she discovered the other documents which she had innocently asked his assistance in translating before the hero translated them for her.

Lise only wants to find her mother. The hero, Salleh, wants, more than anything in the world, to protect the woman he has come to love. However, his life is further complicated when his father is arrested for 'collaborating with foreigners' in his business dealings and the hero has to return to his family duties but not before he and Lise have some private time together. Before they do, however, in a hair raising confrontation with Borman, Abdullah and the hired killer, Lise survives to be reunited with her mother.

She also meets her step father. The aunt and uncle also meet her parents. When Salleh has to return to the family business Lise, her aunt and uncle are on their own in Kuala Lumpur. She copes and being the strong and resilient person she is, takes advantage of the time to visit the city and its environs.

And this being a romance Lise returns home to Montreal where she resumes her career among her friends and with her Samoyed, Waha.

Salleh is able to help his father resume the direction of the company in Kuala Lumpur and is sent back to Montreal to become manager of the family's north American office there.

Putting their unpleasant experiences in Malaysia behind them, Lise and Salleh plan a life together, with the Samoyed, Waha, in Montreal.

LESSON 24 continued

Lets Put It All Together

Synopsis of "Aminata of Casamance"

My novel is set in contemporary Dakar, Senegal; Paris, France; Burssels, Belgium and Montreal, Quebec, Canada. The story concerns an exceptionally beautiful metisse (French/Senegalese) woman who was the first ethnic to be hired in Rome and Paris as a super model. Through savings and advantageous marriages she finds herself very weathly. Weathly enough, in fact, to open boutiques in Dakar, Brussels, Paris and Montreal. Because of an incident during the Second World War in which French soldiers raided her village, killing her parents, she grows up vowing to avenge their deaths. Through the years she is able to find the leader involved and find enough of his doings to blackmail him and others into investing in her businesses.

The story opens in present day Senegal.

From the first time he had seen her, in Paris, she was the only woman he wanted. He had waited for her in more places than he cared to name and now she was the one doing the waiting.

She was exiting her limo, her tall panther-like body gliding toward him in the dimmed lights of the car and the jet. In spite of his resolve to be in complete control, he ran to her.

Bruno van Langtot thought to himself, *I should be gloating.* But he could not bring himself to feel anything. This wasn't like the other times when he had taken revenge. His financial power had always protected him. He guessed this might just be the one exception. She was Aminata of Casamance, Senegal, West Africa. The woman created fright in the strongest men. She had power over many people.

But as of now, he had her number, he and her other enemies.

Erica Young was 35, medium brown skinned, medium height, slim. She wore one of her own designs from an Aminata Internationale boutique.

The possibility of her ascent to this stage in the fashion world of Paris had been next to nil when she arrived there ten years before, green from the all-black city of Mound Bayou, Mississippi, not even speaking the language. She had been laughed out of more fashion houses than she cared to remember when some one had told her about Aminata Internationale.

Now, taking a last sip of champagne, she placed her flute on the tablet in front of her in the first class section of the Air France flight, she contemplated how she would reap her revenge.

LESSON 24 continued

Lets Put It All Together

The person Aminata had saved, now vowed to destroy her.

G. G. Goyer was gloating because she had just learned that the woman known as Aminata of Casamance was coming to Montreal! It was far off her route. This pleased G.G. no end. Montreal was her turf. G.G. rubbed her exquisite, well-manicured hands together with glee. I'm ready for her! After all these years!

The stretched limo slid slowing down Clarke Avenue in Westmount. Prince Albert Antoine Phillipe de Vileneuve was the lone passenger. He was en route to Aminata's newest acquisition where her first Montreal board meeting was to be held.

She wanted to surprise him! *Too late for you,* he thought and snarled, "We're onto you."

Yannick Fleming took another gulp of the personal blend coffee he drank black every morning. He sat on the terrace of his palatial early 19th Century country home in Ste. Agathe, Quebec, Canada. He attempted to dress to reflect his position as a bank manager. He had made it.

He thought, *only forty-eight hours. Lord almighty. Only forth-eight more hours and my life will be changed forever. Aminata Internationale will be history.*

Lo wasn't called "The Snake" for nothing. He could easily slither out this window and down the fire escape without being seen. He had done such things countless times on several continents. He smiled. He could do this job among the glitter of Montreal, fade back into the shadows and be continents away before anyone would be the wiser.

This assignment was a piece of cake. What a waste to kill her but a contract was a congtract and that was his business. He wasn't known as "The Snake" for nothing. And Aminata of Casamance hadn't a chance against him.

However, they all had underestimated Aminata. With the help of her fiancé and her own knowledge of her enemies, she triumphs to live happily ever after.

LESSON 24 continued

Lets Put It All Together

The synopsis from "Charlotte's Tree," a saga.

I begin my story in 1827 when the heroine, Charlotte Lee, is seven years old. Mississippi had joined the Union only eight years before. Previous to that marginal white land owners had lost all or most of their slaves because of various economic setbacks. Consequently, alongside slavery, there existed small free black communities here and there, where the inhabitants lived precarious lives and earned their living as best they could.

Charotte lives on the edg e of the village, in the black section, with her aunt Iona who makes a living as a midwife. Serious tension has been growing between whites and blacks for several months and the tiny free black community is on edge. When someone knocks on their cabin door at dawn the woman and child freeze in fright. It's only their sponsor's chauffeur whose wife is having a baby. Later that day, the girl gets a baptism in life's realities, her first day on the job, as her aunt's helper. She becomes a full fledged midwife at 13.

Charlotte Lee and her aunt are befriended and sponsored by a sympathetic white doctor, Joel Blaylock and his wife, Alicia. They are obliged to 'help out' at the doctor's home whenever the doctor's bitter, eccentric and hateful wife thinks she needs them.

Charlotte learns a little reading and writing with their sponsor's daughter, Mary Ann, and at the church school run by the local black preacher. At 14, she is raped by two white men one morning on her solitary way to deliver a baby outside the village.

When her aunt dies she is alone until she marries a free black from Atlanta. Her husband, William Ford, owns a blacksmith shop, a harness shop and is an ordained Methodist minister. His mother was a seamstress: his father a blacksmith. William's father had tolerated his son's ambition to become a Methodist minister but cautioned him: "Ain't no nigger ever made no living preaching to other niggers. Y'all better learn a trade." William learned his father's trade.

William's sponsor is an eccentric, extremely wealthy white mystery man. William Ford is haughty, proud and 'uppity', but local whites leave him alone because his sponsor is 'powerful'. However, William is murdered several years later by 'unknowns'. Charlotte takes over the businesses and with their children: three boys and three girls, successfully runs them until the Civil War.

Alicia Blaylock is killed accidently and the doctor's only son is killed in the war. His daughter, Mary Ann, marries and goes to live in New Orleans.

All three of Charlotte's sons return from the war and become Methodist ministers. Her

LESSON 24 continued

Lets Put It All Together

daughters marry and go off. She becomes a strong force in the African Methodist church in Crystal Springs, Mississippi. One son, Robert, becomes pastor where his father had been the church's first black minister.

Robert marries Angeline Pierre, a free chalf-Choctaw girl. Her father, Jasper, is a carpenter. Using forged 'sponsors' papers, Jasper had brought his enfant daughter to live with his free midwife mother, Ma Pierre, in a nearby village. She passes her metier to Angeline. They had come from an Indian village in Louisiana where Jasper's young Indian wife died when the child, Angeline, was born.

Angeline has attended the church school for a few years. She meets Robert Ford when he comes to their church to preach. Robert invites himself to her and her father's home for dinner. They marry shortly afterwards.

During the early years of their marriage, Robert's churches took him to many places. Their fourth child was named Carrie Elisabeth. Carrie E was tomboyish to the point of embarrassing her family. From an early age she preferred her brother's clothes to her won. Their pants allowed her to ride horseback astride instead of the sedate, ladylike, side saddle. She could out ride, out hunt all thre of her brothers as well as out shoot all of them. It was she who skinned the animals they shot and cured the hides. Yet, she learned to play the church organ so well that she was called upon to play it for her father's services. While she didn't becme a midwife, she became Charlotte's favorite grandchild.

Although retired when Carie E married Alex Barbette, Charlotte delivered their first child. She lived withher favorite granddaughter for weeks on end.

Alex Barbette's father, Henri, had run away from home near Port-au-Prince, Haiti at 12 to go to sea. He was captured and sold into slavery in Mississipi when his ship docked at mobile, Alabama toward the end of slavery in the United States. It was a time when slave owners were almost paranoid about keeping their slaves and slave catchers were becoming wealthy from 'catching' slaves by any means possible.

Alex's father was married to a slave girl, Elly, who died soon after emancipation. Henri Barbette struggled to bring up Alex and a sister, Sarah. Henri dies of sunstroke when Alex is 16. Alex goes towork on a sugar cane plantatin in Louisiana. He migrates to Crystal Springs where he meets the Ford family. He becomes part of the family, attending church services with them, and courts one of the girls, Ida. He rents a farm and shocks the family by asking to marry Carrie E instead of Ida!

LESSON 24 continued

Lets Put It All Together

Throughout this time Charlotte is there, supervising, counselling, helping and arranging things. When she's 82, Alex and Carrie E decide to move to the Delta. Charlotte goes along to help with the children, wagons and buggy. After seeing that they're properly settled, she and one of her grandsons hitch up her buggy and she takes the reins on the first lap of their return to Crystal Springs.

Ever read the blurbs on romance novel jackets? Style your synopsis after these. What are the highlights of **Your Romance Novel?**

Highlight. Never write out the ending.

Write a 1000 word synopsis of **Your Romance Novel.**

Use your software to count your words or write below.

LESSON 25

LET'S TRY FOR SUCCESS

Your first page has to be a grabber. So, having carefuly developed your plot, conflict, sexual tension, *tags* and characters, you are ready to develop your first paragraph.

Remember what grabbed your attention and interest in the stories and books you like.

How did the author hold your interest in the first few pages? To jog your memory, reread Chapter One of the novels you listed in Lesson 2, page 3.

How did the stories develop your interest?

List what held your attention.

Here is the first paragraph from: "Charlotte's Tree."

It was still dark. The rough, weathered boards of Iona's small cabin sheltered damp night shadows, and, from the scrub-grass clearing around it, nearing-end-of-night mist rose roward the haze shrouded full moon. The last edges of deep sleep drifted from Iona's resisting body, lying softly mounded beneath a faded quilt. Rough croaker sacking covered the uneven cornshuck mattress softening the hard, narrow, wooden-slat bed. From the deep recesses of her age-wearied inner sigh, Iona sensed the coming light. Half-formed dreams and time-dimmed memories drifted through her sleep-drugged thoughts converging on the fact of yesterday's thirteen year-old mulatto patient, her features and voice frozen in fear, lifeblood streaming from her child/woman depths. A beating by her irate father, enraged that the overseer had raped and impregnated his daughter, powerless to proetst, had loosened her slight body's hold on the tiny life, testament to her shame, rushing it to early birth/death on a river of blood that had not ceased its flowing until her eyes fluttered closed and her spirit fled. There was nothing Iona could do but hold her close, easing her dying with her own pain.

The first paragraph from: "Whispers in the Snow."

"You made it!"

Danielle Garon ran her hand through her short black curly hair. "I now. Thank goodness the grader came along and cleared our road. Otherwise even suki wouldn't have been able to get out of our driveway," she said out of breath. She had broken into a trot in order to arrive in the studio on time.

LESSON 25 continued

The first two paragraphs from "Whispers on the Sea."

Suddenly the slate sky turned into dark, heavy clouds that seemed to have come from nowhere. Captain Custairs went below and donned his raincoat. When he returned topside Cargo was running along the right side of the yacht in a frenzy of excited barking. When Captain Custairs looked toward the horizon he was riveted by the sight of a skiff barely visible on the water.

He reached for the binoculars always at hand. A human! In the bottom of the skiff an anonymous mass lay huddled. He carefully manouvered the yacht alongside the skiff and secured it to the yacht with a stout rope. In the meanwhile Cargo ran back and forth along side of the yacht barking more than ever.

List below what held your attention in the three examples above.

Would you want to read further?

LESSON 26

THE CLIMAX

The climax of **Your Romance Novel** occurs when the conflict is at its highest point. Resolution follows shortly after. Make the tension of your story build up naturely to the climax.

How can you do this masterfully? How can you lead up to this? Have you designed ways to make your hero/heroine suffer?

Return to your **Plot**.

Have you done everything possible to heighten the conflicts and make the climax more powerful?

Write the climax. Make it glow!

LESSON 27

Don't bore your readers by dragging the resolution on and on!

Work on an upbeat ending, the stronger the better. True romance novels usually **ALWAYS** have a happy ending. If **Your Romance Novel** is a saga, did you end it where a sequel could begin?

Write several possible endings. Choose the one you think most interesting.

LESSON 28

KEEP YOUR READER IN MIND

What are your readers expectations? Are they reading for pure enjoyment (escapism)? Romance reading is certainly this.

Why don't you take a moment to list examples based on what your readers expect and decide if you are giving it to them?

Again, let's look at "Whispers in the Sand." In this contemporary romance novel, my readers expect a spunky female documentary film producer who is eager when her work takes her to an exotic land full of sexy women and exotic handsome men, full of intrigue and suspense. They expect her to triumph. That is what they get. The story is about a beautiful documentary film producer who gets her first big break only to have a member of her film crew commit an unforgivable crime. She has been seduced by a handsome, debonair diplomat of the country. She flees the country after the crime. He pursues her to her country and manages to recapture her heart.

Write your example.

LESSON 29

GETTING THE DETAILS STRAIGHT. RESEARCH.

Don't rely on your memory, even small scene blunders can distract from **Your Romance Novel.**

Do the groundwork necessary to get your facts straight. Don't have a telephone or cars in an 18th Century historical romance. Make sure you are correct about the kind of transportation and the correct terms used to describe them were in use at the time and place your story takes place. Get the facts right. A few history books from your local library and some research on the Internet can be very valuable.

LESSON 30

THE TITLE

Look at your setting, hero/heroine character sketch, general plot, conflict, the sexual tension and *tags,* what your story is about, and your synopsis. Underline the key words or phrases that might capture the mood of **Your Romance Novel.** Could you choose any of these as a good title? Write them down to look at later.

The title for "Whispers in the Sand' was chosen after I wrote the following:

Lorraine suddenly felt as though she were back in the 12th Century as she looked at the curiously dressed people accompanying the endless line of loaded camels and listened to the whoosh, whoosh of the camel's hooves. Their hooves sounded like "Whispers in the Sand,"she thought.

Lesson 30a. Using words and phrases, try combining them to see what you come up with.

Lesson 30b. Still having trouble? Write down more words and phrases. Remember you

Lesson 30b. continued

can also consult your computer's Thesaurus. Look up synonyms. Play with them below or on your computer.

LESSON 31

HERE IS WHERE I BOW OUT

Now it's up to you to write. Turn on your computer, your printer, screen and go for it. You have a clear idea of **Your Romance Novel:** your plot, your characters, your theme, the sexual tension, *tags* and conflict. Unlike those other writers who are still stumbling through writer's block and blank screen syndrome, your chances of writing a salabhle romance novel are much improved. *GOOD LUCK!*

Write to me if you need further instructions at my e-mail address: laflorya@total.net

****

Some Helpful Tips:

Writer's Block.

Tip One: When writer's block strikes, and it surely will, try writing: 1) How you feel about writer's block. 2) What the weather is like and how it makes you feel. 3) What you see in front of your window and how you feel about it. 4) What color telephone you have and why you chose it. 5) Write for ten minutes.

Tip Two: 1) Imagine you are walking down a street, near the corner. 2) Imagine what is around the corner. 3) Let your imagination run wild. (For example: If you live in the Canadian north or Alaska you might meet a moose or a bear! What would you do)? If you lived in Chateauguay, Quebec, Canada you might meet a skunk, a rabbit, a racoon or a squirrel. What would you do?

Having Dialogue Problems?

Having trouble with dialogue? Write two pages of only dialogue between any of your characters, keeping in mind that dialogue:
1. Reveals what has taken place in the past
2. Moves your plot
3. Suggests future events
4. Reveals character through the words of other characters
5. Heightens and intensifies mood
6. Describes and contributes to settings
7. In a romance novel, gives sexual undertones
8. In a romance novel, reveals passion
9. Conveys state of mind.

Some Helpful Tips continued

Having trouble telling a certain part of your story?

How would you tell it to your:

Mother?

Maiden aunt?

Sister?

A five year old child?

Your husband?

Your father?

Your brother?

Some Helpful Tips continued

A stranger   (Female)?

A stranger (male)?

A male friend?

A female friend?

Appendix I

Some Reading

Koontz, D. R. (1981).   How To Write Best Selling Fiction.
Cincinnati: Writer's Digest Books.

MacCampbell, D. (1978). The Writing Business. New York: Crown Publishers.

Sloane, W. (1979). The Craft of Writing. New York: Norton.

Lowery, M. M. (1983). How to Write Romance Novels That Sell. New York. Rawson
Associates.

Barnhart, H. S. (1984). Writing Romance Fiction For Love and Money. Cincinnati. Writer's
Digest Books.

Krull, K. (1989). 12 Keys to Writing Books That Sell. Cincinnati. Writer's Digest Books.

Hull, R. (1984). How to Write How-to Books and Articles. Cincinnati. Writer's Digest Books.

Rico, G. L. (1983). Writing the Natural Way. Los Angeles, J. P. Tarcher, Inc.

Clark, B. (1983). Writer's Resource Guide. Cincinnati. Writer's Digest Books.

Collier, O. And Leighton, F. S. (1986). How to Write and Sell Your First Novel. Cincinnati. Writer's Digest Books.

Block, L. (1979). Writing the Novel: From Plot to Print.

Adams, J. (1984). How to Sell What your Write. New York. G. P. Putnam's Sons.

Kelly, V. (1986). How to Write Erotica. New York. Harmony Books.

Buchman, D. D. and Groves, S. (1987). The Writer's Guide to Manuscript Formats. Cincinnati. Writer's Digest Books.

Landau, S. I. And Bogus, R. J. (1977). The Doubleday Roget's Thesaurus in Dictionary Form. New York. Doubleday & Company, Inc.

Prestwood, E. (1984). The Creative Writer's Phrase-Finder. ETC Publications. Palm Springs.

Paludan, Eve. (1996). Romance Writer's Pink Pages. Prima Publishing Company, P.O. Box 1260, Rocklin, CA 95677.

Falk, K. (1999). Ho , To Write A Romance For The New Markets. Genesis Press, Inc,.315 Third Avenue North, Columbus, MS 39701. Web Page: http://www.genesis-press.com

Nelson, V. (1993). On Writer's Block, Houghton Mifflin Company, 215 Park Avenue South, New York 10003.

****

Romance Publishers and their lines: (Copy their Internet addresses from their book covers which you will read in bookstores, pharmacies, department and variety stores, etc.

Here's a partial list

Avon Books, Ballantine Books, Bantam Books, Berkley/Jove, Dell Publishing Company, Doubleday Publishing Company, E. P. Dutton, Fawcett Books, Harlequin Books, The New American Library, Warner Books, Zebra Books, Genesis Press, Inc.

Appendix II

Romance Periodicals

Affaire de Coeur
Publisher, Louise Snead
3976 Oak Hill Road
Oakland, CA 94605-4931
Telephone: (510) 569-5675
FAX: (510) 632-8868
e-mail: sseven@msn.com
www.affairedecoeur.com

Romantic Times
Kathryn Falk, Lady of Barrow
55 Bergen Street
Brooklyn, New York 11201
Telephone: (718) 237-1097
FAX: (718) 624-4231
Web Site: www.romantictimes.com
e-mail: info@romantictimes.com

Romance Writers Report
Romance Writers of America
Suite 315, 13700 Veterans Memorial Drive
Houston, Texas 77014

Romance Books and Reviews
3744 Charlemagne
Long Beach, California 90808

Appendix III

Publishers Weekly
Subscription Department
R.R. Bowker Company
P.O. Box 13710
Philadelphia, Pennsylvania 19101

Appendix IV

Writer's Digest
Subscription Service
Box 2123
Harlan, IA 51593
www.writersdigest.com

Printed in the United States
1283300002BA/37

9 780595 149360